MY FAVORITE DOG

SIBERIAN HUSKIES

by Mark & Solomon Shulman
Dog Expert: Beth Adelman, MS
Former editor, *American Kennel Club Gazette*

Kaleidoscope
Minneapolis, MN

The Quest for Discovery Never Ends

This edition first published in 2021 by Kaleidoscope Publishing, Inc.

For information regarding permission, write to
Kaleidoscope Publishing, Inc.
6012 Blue Circle Drive
Minnetonka, MN 55343

Library of Congress Control Number
2020936244

ISBN
978-1-64519-461-3 (library bound)
978-1-64519-463-7 (ebook)

Printed in the United States of America.

FIND ME IF YOU CAN!

Bigfoot lurks within one of the images in this book. It's up to you to find him!

TABLE OF CONTENTS

Introduction

Here Comes a Siberian Husky!

Alan's family had moved to a new city. He was lonely. A smart, friendly dog would be his new best friend. First, Alan had to convince his parents.

"No barking dogs," said his mom. "And not too big."

"He has to like the cold and snow," said his dad.

They read about different **breeds**. They talked to dog owners. They learned that a Siberian Husky would be perfect. Alan already had a name picked out.

At breakfast time, Alan hurried downstairs. Thor was waiting for him!

Chapter 1

The Story of Siberian Huskies

The Chukchi people still live in northern Russia.

Many centuries ago, the first Siberian Huskies were bred by the Chukchi people of Siberia. Siberia is in northeastern Russia. It is very cold there. The Chukchi had to wander far from home to hunt for food. Their dogs helped them travel by dogsled. The dogs were not too big, so they could run long distances. The sled dogs' thick fur could stand the cold. The Chukchi also needed dogs who were smart and loyal.

Siberian Huskies were just what they needed. Siberians are strong and have lots of energy. They're not huge and heavy, so they can run fast. They can pull dogsleds in freezing snow for a long time. Sled dog teams carried people and supplies. The dogs also became part of people's families.

Siberian Huskies first came to America in 1908. They pulled sleds for fur traders in Alaska. They helped deliver mail. They won a lot of races. People became interested in these amazing dogs!

In the winter of 1925, many people in Nome, Alaska, were getting sick. There was an **epidemic** of a disease called **diphtheria**. The medicine that could save their lives was about 675 miles (1,085 km) away, near the big city of Fairbanks. In the winter, the only way to get to Nome was by dogsled.

A **relay** of 20 Siberian Husky dogsled teams began the Great Race of Mercy. Their goal was to bring medicine to the people of Nome as quickly as they could. For six days, the teams sped over mountains and across ice. They could barely see in the blinding snow and powerful winds.

THE IDITAROD

The most famous dogsled race is the Iditarod (eye-DIT-a-rod). The race covers part of the trail Togo and Balto followed. Each year, teams of 14 dogs race. They often face very cold and snowy weather. The trail can be more than 1,000 miles (1,600 km) long. The fastest winner finished in a bit more than eight days.

In 1925, sled dogs Togo (far left) and Balto (with musher Gunnar Kaasen) helped save the people of Nome.

A famous **musher** named Leonhard Seppala traveled 91 miles (146 km) in a blizzard. That was the longest part of the relay. He gave all the credit to Togo, the Siberian who led his team. Gunnar Kaasen ran the last part of the relay. It was 53 miles (85 km). His lead Siberian Husky was named Balto. The medicine they brought saved the people of Nome!

Back at Alan's house, Thor soon felt like part of the family. Huskies are social dogs. That means they make friends quickly. They don't like to be left alone. They'll happily bounce up to someone new, hoping to play.

Renee lives in Alan's neighborhood. Some dogs make her nervous, but not Thor.

"Don't worry, he doesn't bark," says Alan.

Renee throws a stick. Thor jumps high over a bush to **retrieve** it. He quickly brings it back and licks her hand. They're friends already.

"I think Thor would not be a very good guard dog," says Renee, and they laugh.

WHERE SIBERIAN HUSKIES COME FROM

Chukchi Sea

RUSSIA

ALASKA

The Chukchi Peninsula, Siberia, Russia

Gulf of Alaska

Bering Sea

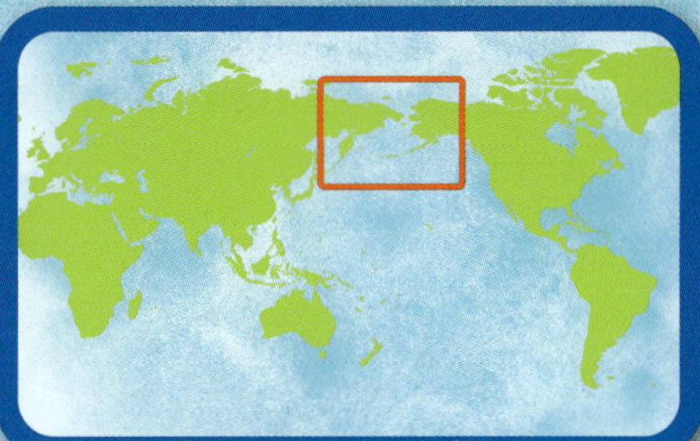

FUN FACT

Siberian Huskies are excellent jumpers. They can easily leap over low fences. Husky owners make sure backyard fences are more than 6 feet (1.83 m) high.

Chapter 2

Looking at a Siberian Husky

Many people first notice a Siberian's eyes. Thor's blue eyes are kind and intelligent. He has a bright look that almost feels like winter. Most Siberians have blue eyes, but they can have brown or hazel eyes, too.

Thor holds his head up high and alert. His ears stand up in pointed triangles. It looks like he's always hearing something new and interesting. His ears are thick and furry, even on the inside. That's helpful when it's freezing outside!

FUN FACT

Some Siberians have one blue eye and one brown eye.

THE SIBERIAN HUSKY

MALES

HEIGHT*:
21–23.5 in. (53–60 cm)

WEIGHT:
45–60 lbs. (20–27 kg)

FEMALES

HEIGHT*:
20–22 in. (51–56 cm)

WEIGHT:
35–50 lbs. (16–23 kg)

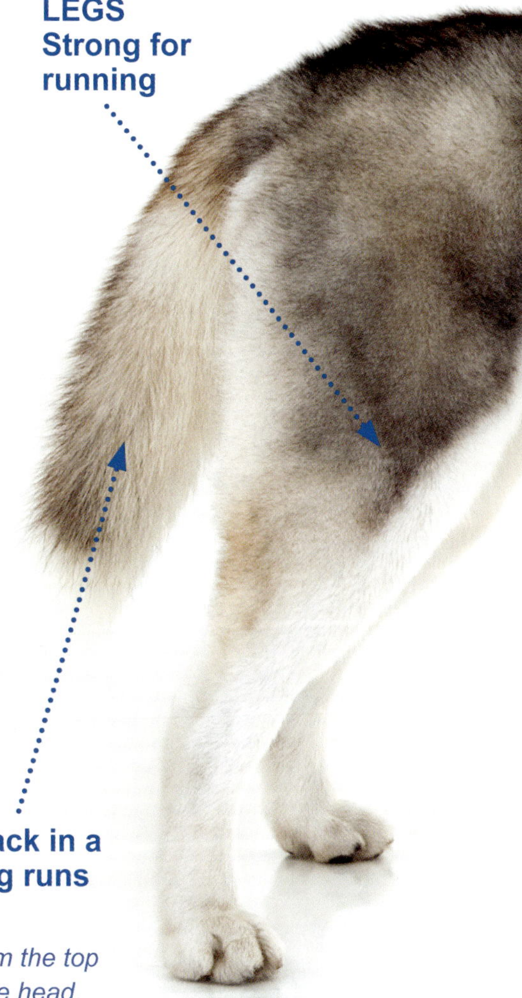

LEGS
Strong for running

TAIL
Carried over the back in a curve when the dog runs

**The height of a dog is measured from the top of the shoulder, not from the top of the head.*

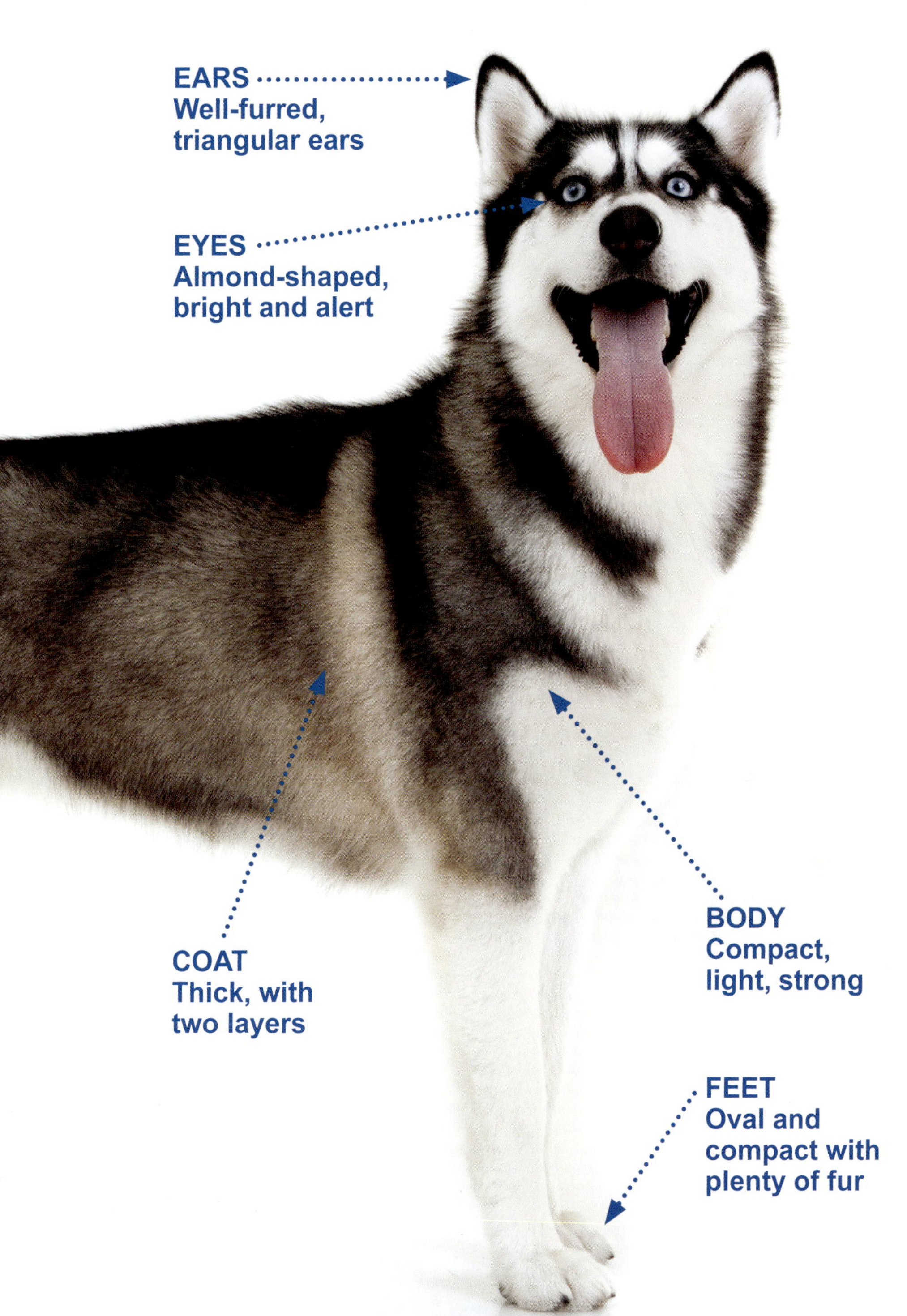
EARS
Well-furred, triangular ears
EYES
Almond-shaped, bright and alert
COAT
Thick, with two layers
BODY
Compact, light, strong
FEET
Oval and compact with plenty of fur

From ears to paws, Siberians are light and graceful. When they run, they don't look like they're working hard.

Double coats of hair cover their strong bodies. The top layer is short and straight. The **undercoat** is soft and thick. This protects them in a freezing blizzard, and it also keeps out the summer heat.

Alan and his family live in a state

FUN FACT

A Siberian's nose can be black, brown, or even light tan. In the winter, some Siberians can have a pink-streaked "snow nose."

where it gets very cold in the winter. Thor's coat is perfect for that kind of weather.

Thor has a black and white coat. A Siberian's fur can be any shade of black, white, gray, tan, or a reddish color called sable.

FACE FACTS

Some Siberians are all one color. But many have unique markings of light and dark on their faces. They can have many patterns on their bodies, too. You could say that no two Siberians look alike!

Chapter 3

Meet a Siberian Husky!

Siberians were bred to be runners. They need plenty of exercise every day. They also need to be someplace where they won't run away. Thor is always eager to run and play. Alan takes him out to their fenced-in yard. They also visit the dog park.

When they are out on a winter trail, Siberians dig holes in the snow to sleep in. Even when there's no snow, Thor loves to dig in the yard. Alan's family gave him a big pile of sand to dig in, so he can have a good time.

When Thor wants to go for a walk, he brings Alan his leash in his mouth. Thor loves to run, and he might dash out the door. So Alan has trained him to sit and wait while he puts on the leash.

With Alan holding the leash, the dog nearly pulls the boy down the street. Renee waves as they go by. "Hey, Alan," she calls. "Who's walking who?"

Thor is an active dog, and he is super smart. He makes up his own games to keep himself busy. But sometimes he keeps busy by chewing on things in the house! Alan makes sure he has plenty of toys to chew on.

Thor loves his family time, too. When he's indoors, he settles down and sits quietly with the family. Alan gently pets Thor during reading or screen time.

The friendly Siberian rarely barks or growls. But he does like to howl sometimes. Everyone laughs when Thor joins in the music and sings along.

STAY COOL!

Siberians don't like the heat. In the summer, Alan and Renee fill up a plastic kiddie pool for Thor. They all have a great time splashing and staying cool! Thor stays inside in the air conditioning during the hottest part of the day.

Chapter 4

Caring for a Siberian Husky

In the spring and fall, Thor's thick undercoat falls out in big clumps. When this happens, Alan takes him outside and brushes him every day. He uses a special rake that gently removes the old hair.

When Thor is not **shedding**, Alan brushes him once a week. He uses a metal comb with wide teeth. The comb moves easily through Thor's double coat. Thor likes the feel of the comb. He rolls over. Alan can comb Thor's belly, too!

Alan's dad or mom trim Thor's nails once a month with a special tool. Siberians have small, tight feet. Having long nails can hurt them.

Thor doesn't fuss when they trim his nails. They give him special treats to let him know he's a good boy!

Even at feeding time, Thor is no problem. He only eats when he's hungry. In fact, he'll walk away from his bowl when he gets full.

Thor's **veterinarian** recommended a top-quality dog food, with plenty of protein and some fat, too. This is like the Huskies' diet in the frozen north. Alan chooses foods that include fish, chicken, or beef.

When Thor was a puppy, he ate three times a day. Now that he's older, he eats twice a day.

DOGS NEED CHECK-UPS

Thor goes to the veterinarian twice a year. The veterinarian checks to make sure he is healthy. She weighs him to see if he is fat or skinny or just right. He also goes to the veterinarian if he is not feeling well. How can Alan tell? A sick dog might eat less. Or play less. Or sleep more. Or act grouchy.

It's been a long day for Alan and Thor. They ran and played. They practiced some tricks. They went for a couple of walks.

Alan lies down in bed and Thor lies on the floor nearby. He curls up in a circle with his tail over his nose. Even in a warm house, Thor's **instinct** is to protect himself from the cold.

Alan's parents tell him that he's been a good friend for Thor. Alan knows that, and so does Thor.

Siberian Huskies served in the Air Force during World War II. They were used to find pilots whose planes crashed in the cold north. Some of these dogs learned how to jump out of airplanes using parachutes!

Huskies know how to sleep in the snow. Curling up helps them keep warm.

BEYOND THE BOOK

After reading the book, it's time to think about what you learned. Try the following exercises to jumpstart your ideas.

RESEARCH

FIND OUT MORE. There is so much more to find out about Siberian Huskies. Visit the American Kennel Club's site to research Siberians. Or look for a Siberian Husky Club in your area. You can meet other people who love your favorite breed!

CREATE

TIME FOR ART. As the book says—and the pictures show—Siberians can have many patterns and colors of hair. Get some markers and paper and have some fun drawing Siberians with different hair designs. How creative can you be? Look at other pictures of Siberians online to find more ideas for your drawings.

DISCOVER

LOTS OF BREEDS. This book is about your favorite dog breed. But there are hundreds more around the world. Visit the AKC site or those of other dog organizations. What other breeds can you discover? Which breeds are related to your favorite? What is the most interesting new breed you have discovered?

GROW

HELP OUT! Animal shelters can be great places to volunteer. Contact a shelter near you and find out if you can help. Or can your family donate food or gear to help rescue dogs? Find out why dogs end up in shelters. Is there anything you can do to help them find homes?

Visit www.ninjaresearcher.com/4613 to learn how to take your research skills and book report writing to the next level!

SEARCH LIKE A PRO
Learn about how to use search engines to find useful websites.

FACT OR FAKE?
Discover how you can tell a trusted website from an untrustworthy resource.

TEXT DETECTIVE
Explore how to zero in on the information you need most.

SHOW YOUR WORK
Research responsibly—learn how to cite sources.

WRITE

GET TO THE POINT
Learn how to express your main ideas.

PLAN OF ATTACK
Learn prewriting exercises and create an outline.

DOWNLOADABLE REPORT FORMS

Further Resources

BOOKS

Boykin, Brittany. *Siberian Husky Training: The Ultimate Guide.* Sheridan, WY: CAC Publishing, 2018.

Clutton-Brock, Juliet. *Dog.* New York: DK Publishing, 2014.

Sirota, Lyn. *Siberian Huskies (All About Dogs).* New York: Weigl Publishing, 2018.

Warren, Cat, and Patricia Wynne. *What the Dog Knows: Young Reader's Edition.* New York: Simon & Schuster Publishing, 2019.

WEBSITES

Factsurfer.com gives you a safe, fun way to find more information.

1. Go to www.factsurfer.com.
2. Enter "Siberian Huskies" into the search box and click 🔍
3. Select your book cover to see a list of related websites.

Glossary

breeds: different types of dogs; dogs of the same breed have the same traits.

diphtheria: a dangerous disease of the neck and throat.

epidemic: a disease that affects many, many people.

instinct: knowledge or behavior that an animal has from birth.

musher: a person who drives a dogsled.

protein: the ingredient in food that builds muscle and makes energy.

relay: a long race where each member of a team runs just one small part.

retrieve: to bring something back.

shedding: when a lot of hair falls out naturally.

undercoat: the layer of hair that is shorter than the top layer and closest to the dog's skin.

veterinarian: a doctor for animals.

Index

PHOTO CREDITS

The images in this book are reproduced through the courtesy of: Alamy: Konstantin Shevtsov 6. iStock.com: Kal9 4. Shutterstock: Eric Isselee 3, 17T; Kirk Geisler 7; Troutnut 8; Everett Historical 9T; Anurak Pongpatimet 10, 21, 24; uf4-tol 12; Melinda Nagy 13; Natliya Sbodnikova 14; ThanesOp 15; Evgeny Haritonov 16; Odua Images 17B; Paisit Teeraphatsakool 17R; Frenzl 18; Kazlova Iryna 18; Nejron Photo 19; Pixel-Spot 20; Konstantin Zaykov 22; Parilov 23; Sergey Bessudov 25; Torcik 26; Janne Liuski 27. **Cover and page 1:** Pixel-Shot/Shutterstock (cover); Nazarovsergey/Shutterstock (p1). Paw prints: Maximillian Laschon/Shutterstock.

About the Author

The writing team of Mark and Solomon Shulman have more than 160 books between them. Their books cover subjects ranging from football to dogs. They live in New York City. Mark grew up with a real boy named Alan who had a real Siberian Husky named Thor.